CAPTURED BY
THEIR PAST

Order this book online at www.trafford.com
or email orders@trafford.com

Most Trafford titles are also available at major online book retailers.

Print information available on the last page.

ISBN: 978-1-4120-6728-7 (sc)

Trafford rev. 02/19/2021

 www.trafford.com

North America & international
toll-free: 844-688-6899 (USA & Canada)
fax: 812 355 4082

The Characters of this play are:

John Brown: A writer. Sixty years old
John Brown Jr: His son
Charles Brown: His other son.
Linda Donaldson: John Brown's Jr wife
Edward Mc Donald: The Butler.
Harry Whitehall: The editor.
Miss Jefferson: Harry Whitehall´s secretary.
Frank Robertson: The doctor.
Jason Parker: John Brown's neighbour.
Reginald Johnson: The policeman.
Mary Robertson: John Brown's maid.
George Edwards: The prosecutor.
Michael Smith: A friend of Mr Brown and the main
character of the play.

INDEX:

CHAPTER 1: A MURDER

My name is Michael Smith. I am sixty years old and I am married. I live in Manchester. My wife is called Mary. I am a lawyer and she is my secretary. We have two children, Mike and Philip. Mike is thirty-eight and Philip is thirty-five. Both are married. Mike is a dentist and Philip is an engineer. Both have a daughter and a son.
Everything happened one year ago. I was in London for business and I decided to visit an old friend whom I had not seen for a long time.
He was called John Brown and we had met at school and continued studying together until I met my wife and moved to Manhester.In spite of the distance, we had met quite often, the last time was at his wife's funeral, two years before.
He was not very tall, he was sixty years old, brown-eyed, not very fat and a dark-haired man. He had two sons, John and Charles, who lived in Liverpool. He was a writer and he had had a lot of success in his career. He had always written mystery novels. The main character in his books was a middle-aged detective, whose name was James Parker. His most successful novel was *The Pearl's mystery*. He liked reading mystery novels, especially from Agatha Christie. He had all her books and had read them many times. The book he liked most was
The murder of Roger Ackroyd. He was retired now, and could live without writing, but he liked it very much, so he had started another novel. He had written more than eighty during all his life. He lived in a big house with a garden at the front and another one at the back. When I got there, his maid opened the door. I had never seen her before; she had dark hair and big green eyes. She was young, about twenty three years old I thought. The one I had met was older, with blond hair, blue eyes, and taller.

- Good morning, can I help you?
- Yes, please. Could you tell Mr Brown that Mr Smith is here?
- Of course sir, follow me, please.
- Thank you very much.
- Could you wait here for a moment, please?
- Of course.

She led me to the living room. I waited for him there. It was very big, with some paintings of London on the wall at the front, and photos of different places he had visited with his wife and alone around the world. He had been to India, Greece, Italy and Spain among many other countries. He also had painted landscapes from England and Scotland. Another of his hobbies was going for a walk on Sundays, and visit different places from London like the National Gallery, Covent Garden or the Westminster Abbey.

On the left side of the room, there was a door through which you passed to the kitchen, and then to a bathroom and, at the end of the corridor, to the library. The bedrooms were upstairs.

While I was waiting in the living room watching the photos, Edward the butler entered and asked me:

- Excuse me sir, my name is Edward, I am the butler, would you like anything to drink?
- No, thanks, I will wait until Mr Brown comes.
- You are welcome; Mr Brown will come in a minute.
- Thank you.

A few minutes later Mr Brown came down. He was happily surprised.

- My goodness! My dearest friend Michael Smith. It has been a long time since we met.
- Two years at least.
- Yes, since Mary's funeral.
- That's right.
- Why haven't you phoned me and said you were coming?

- Because I wanted to surprise you.
- And you have really surprised me!
- How are you?
- I'm fine now. When Mary died, I got very depressed and I decided to travel in order to forget her, but I couldn't.
- What about your sons, have they helped you?
- Yes, they wanted me to go to Liverpool and live with them, but I have always said no. They have their own life there and I don't want to bother them. On the other hand I love London and I do not want to live anywhere else.
- But do they come to visit you very often?
- Yes, they do. By the way, they are here today. They have come this morning and they are going to stay all the weekend here with me.
- Where are they now?
- They have gone to visit some friends and they are going to come back for dinner.
- I see.
- Well, do you want a glass of whisky? My sons have given me one bottle today.
- Thanks. That´s very kind of you, but I don't drink.
- Oh, sorry! I had forgotten.
- Well, I am going to pour one for myself.

Then he served himself a drink, and said:
- Do you want to go to the library?
- Yes, please.

We passed to the long corridor and entered the library. It was very big with two big shelves on the right and on the left all of them full of books. His desk was at the front, with a photo of him, his wife and their children.

Although I had already seen it always surprised me:
- It's very surprising the quantity of books and how big your library is.

- Yes, I do not know the exact number. I have bought many, others have been given to me by my friends or sons as a present and the rest have been written by me.
- By the way, what are you doing now?
- I am writing another novel.
- About murders?
- No, about the trips I have made and the places I have visited.
- I know it will be very good.
- I hope so. When I finish it I will give you one.
- Oh! thank you very much.
- You are welcome.

He drank one gulp, and said:
- How is your family? How is Mary?
- Oh! She is wonderful. She is the best woman in the whole world. She is pretty and intelligent.
- Is she better as a spouse or as a secretary?
- I don't know. She's wonderful in both roles.

He smiled and drank another swallow. I knew it was a sad smile.
- How do you feel?
- Well, I don't feel very well today, the doctor has come this morning and he has advised me I have to take care of myself.
- You shouldn't smoke nor drink.
- That's what the doctor has told me.
- And he is right.
- Yes, but my sons have brought me a bottle of whisky today and I wanted to drink a little.
- Yes, but you should drink moderately.

His sons came while we were talking. The last time I saw them was in their mother's funeral. John was fatter and Charles was a little bit taller. Both were married and lived in Liverpool. Charles was a chemistry teacher. He worked at the university. John was an architect. When they both entered into the room their father said:

4

- Hi boys! , I suppose you know my old friend Mike.
- Of course we know him, it has been a long time since the last time we saw each other, John Jr said.
- Yes, it has been.
- How is your family? Charles asked.
- Everybody is fine, thanks. I have two children and four grandchildren.
- How old are your grandchildren?
- The eldest, Mike, that is Mike's son, is ten years old. The youngest, Mary, that is Philip's daughter, is only six months old.
- They also have children, John said.
- Yes, I have two children and my brother has three, John Jr added.
- You must be absolutely delighted playing with your grandsons, I said to John.
- Yes, they make me laugh.
- Where are your grandchildren now?
- They are staying in Liverpool this weekend, Charles answered.
- They will come next weekend. I am always waiting for the day they come.
- I imagine.
- You must also be absolutely delighted with your grandchildren, John Jr told me.
- Yes I am
- We are both very happy with our grandsons, John said looking at me.
- Yes, we are very lucky of having grandchildren to play with.
- You were both very close friends when you lived and studied here, Charles said.
- Yes, we had a lot of fun.
- Yes, but one day he fell in love with a woman from Manchester and disappeared.
- I only went to Manchester, but we have kept in contact during these years.

- It was only a joke.
- I know that.

The four of us were smiling and talking about the past when Edward the butler entered into the room.

- Dinner is served sir.
- Thank you Edward.
- Well, I have to go to my hotel now.
- No, you are going to have dinner with us.
- I don't want to bother.
- You don't bother, Edward, we will be four for dinner.
- Ok sir.
- All right, I will stay.
- Wonderful!.

A few minutes later we passed to the dinning room. It was very big. There was a long table in the middle, a big shelf full of photos on the left and another one with souvenirs and a painting on the right.

We began having dinner. We were four at the table, John was at the front, his son John on the left, his son Charles on his right and I in front of him. John was very happy and relaxed. He had his closest friend and his sons there and one week later he was going to have his grandsons there too.

We had red wine for the dinner, but John booked his glass of whisky for the cheer. We ate a salad to start and then lamb.

We were at the desserts and John stood up from his chair and said:

- I want to cheer for this special occasion, because today I am having dinner with my two sons and my dearest friend Mike. ¡Cheers!
- ¡Cheers! we all said.

After that, he drank his glass of whisky completely.

- Daddy, you should drink slower, you are not twenty years old anymore, Charles said.
- Yes, I know that, I…Ahh!

- What is happening daddy?
- I cannot breath, my breast!
- John, I said.

He couldn't pronounce any more words. He fell on the floor breaking the glass into thousands of pieces. When we went to help him nothing could be done. I leaned towards him, touched him on his neck and said:

- He is dead.
- What? this can't be true! John said.
- I wish it wasn't true, check by yourselves.
- Oh dear, he is dead, Charles said leaning towards him, touching his neck as well and screaming in horror.
- What has happened? John said.
- I don't know, but the secret must be in this bottle.

I took the bottle and brought it near my nose.

- Oh dear! It has a very disgusting smell.
- Can we smell it? John asked.
- Yes, of course.
- Ugh! it smells very bad, Charles said. It seems arsenic.

I took the bottle, smelled it, put it near the lamp and saw the bottom of it.

- Yes, it seems arsenic to me, and there is some at the bottom.
- We should call the doctor and the police, John said.
- Yes, I think we should.

Then I called the female servant and she came. She screamed in horror.

- Oh dear, Oh dear! , what has happened?
- Mr Brown is dead.
- Dead? why?
- I don't know. Do you know the name of his doctor?
- Yes, his doctor is Frank Robertson.

- Can you give me his telephone number, please?
- Yes, one minute, sir.

She brought the doctor's number and I phoned him.

- Excuse me, is that Frank Robertson?
- Yes, Frank Robertson speaking, who is calling, please?
- Michael Smith speaking, I am a friend of John Brown. I am phoning you from his home. A tragedy has happened; could you come here, please?
- Yes, but what has happened?
- Mr Brown has been killed.
- What? I can't believe it!
- Could you come soon?
- Of course, I will be there in a minute.
- Thank you doctor.
- We should phone the police; John said when I hung up the telephone.
- Yes, I am going to phone them now.

I phoned the police and a few minutes later the doctor was at the house.

- Hi, I am Michael Smith; we have talked by the phone.
- Hello, I am Frank Robertson.

He immediately saw the dead body of Mr Brown lying on the floor. He went towards him and said.

- It's terrible; he told me today that he did not feel very well.
- He has been poisoned.
- Yes, I had already imagined that. We'll make the autopsy and see what has killed him.
- I think the secret must be inside this bottle, and gave the bottle to him.

He took the bottle and put it near his nose.

- Hm, this is arsenic.
- Yes, we had already supposed that.
- He used it very much to kill the victims in his novels, Charles said.

- Yes, and someone has used it to kill him, the doctor said.
- It's very cruel, John answered.
- Yes, it is, I said.
- Why did you suppose it was arsenic? the doctor asked me.
- Well, I am a lawyer and I have had cases of poisoning during my career. Moreover I had read something about it.
- I see.

One minute later the police arrived.

- Hello my name is Reginald Johnson, the inspector said introducing himself.

He was not very tall; he had blue eyes, brown hair, black glasses, a big moustache, brown coat and hat. He seemed a typical English man, with a very good English accent as well.

- I have been informed that there has been a murder in this house.
- Hello my name is Michael Smith. I have phoned you. I was a friend of the victim; I had come today to visit him.
- I am John Brown and this is my brother Charles, he was our father.
- Nice to meet you all. What has exactly happened?
- Mr Brown has been poisoned.
- Someone has put arsenic inside the bottle, We had bought it today for our father. Charles said.
- Why?
- Because he loved whisky.
- Where did you buy it?
- In a shop in Liverpool. We live there.
- Had he drunk before the dinner?
- Yes, one cup after lunch.
- But nothing happened to him.
- No he had just opened it, so there was nothing inside it.

- Where did he drink the whisky?
- In the living room, there.
- Where did he put the bottle then?
- On that table over there.
- Has it been all the time there?
- Yes, till he has brought it with him now for dinner.
- He had drunk a cup while we were talking in the library, and when we went out and were going to the dining room he took the bottle, brought it here and served himself another cup, I said.
- So, anyone could have put the poison before the dinner.
- I suppose so, John said.
- Interesting.
- What are you trying to say? I asked.
- What I am trying to say is that anyone must have put the poison inside the bottle without being noticed at any particular moment during the day.
- Anyone of us?
- Yes, anyone of you, or anyone from the house. By the way could you tell me if your father had enemies? I mean, do you know anyone who wanted him dead? the inspector asked John.
- No, we don't think so. He had many friends.
- Yes, but somebody has killed him, the question is who, why, when and how?

He turned around towards Mary and asked:
- What's your name, please?
- My name is Mary Robertson.
- How long have you been working here?
- One year, sir.
- Who else has entered into the house today?
- Well, many people.
- Has anyone stayed alone near the bottle for more than two minutes?
- I don't know sir.

- Who has stayed for a long time today at the house?
- Anyone except the people who are here just now.
- A-ha, that's interesting. Now, tell me, has he argued with anyone these days?
- I don't know, sir.
- Our father has told us he had a heated discussion with the editor yesterday because he did not want to work for him anymore, John answered.
- Why?
- Because he had found another editorial.
- That is a very strong reason to kill Mr Brown, and, what is the name of the editor by the way?
- Harry Whitehall.
- So he had a good reason to kill Mr Brown. Has he been here today?
- No, he hasn't.
- So that discards him.
- Not necessarily, I said.
- No, not necessarily .By the way, the murderer wore gloves when he put arsenic inside the bottle because there are no fingerprints in it.
- So anyone could have entered into the house, a thief, for example, put the poison inside the bottle and disappear, Charles said.
- In that case the thief should have forced the entrance and would have made some noise, and the entrance is no forced, nothing has disappeared and nobody has heard anything.
- And the thief should have known where the bottle was, John said.
- Yes, he would have taken a big risk, Charles said.
- So if a person from outside the house has not killed Mr Brown that means that anyone from the house has poisoned him.

- And how the person in the house has obtained the poison? I asked.
- I don't know, maybe he or she has gone to buy it.
- Or he or she has an accomplice outside who has bought it and given it to him or her.
- Maybe.

He turned around and looked at me. He had a deep look. He said:
- By the way, you have been here all the evening, is that correct?
- Yes, I have.
- Have you been alone for a moment?
- Yes, when the maid went to tell Mr Brown I was here.
- Near the bottle?
- What are you trying to say?
- I wonder if you had a motive to kill Mr Brown.
- No, I had not, and you are getting me angry with that question, could you tell me exactly what are you hinting at?
- Well, I mean that you have come today, just the same day he gets poisoned.
- Listen to me, I said screaming, I have not killed him, he was a very good friend of mine and I have come here to visit him.
- I am only saying that he has been killed and nobody has come from the outside neither to steal anything nor poison him, so one of you may have killed him.
- Are you telling us that we are suspicious of killing our father? Charles said.
- Maybe.
- For which reason? John said.
- For example, you are his sons, and I suppose you are his inheritors, is that right?
- Yes, we are.

- This house is very nice and I suppose your father was a rich person, wasn't he?
- That's none of your business.
- That's true, that is not of my business, but I suppose he would have made a will.
- Are you telling us we have killed our father to get his money?
- Yes, it could be.
- That's ridiculous.
- It could be ridiculous or not, we'll see. Many murders have been committed by the inheritors to get the victim's fortune. That is a typical motive.
- We have not killed our father, Charles said in a loud voice.
- Maybe not, or....

While we were talking the police was registering the house. One minute later a policeman entered into the dining room and said:

- Excuse me sergeant, could I talk to you for a minute?
- Of course.

They went to a corner of the room and started talking. When they finished he excused himself, left the room and came a few minutes later. When he entered he brought a coat. He stopped in the middle of the room and said:

- Who is the owner of this coat?
- That's my coat, John said, what are you doing with it?
- Sir, you are under arrest. Handcuff him! .Do you want me to read you your rights?
- I know what my rights are, but this is ridiculous, what am I accused of?
- I am going to read them to you anyway. You have the right to keep silent, anything you say can be held against you in a court of law, you have the right to legal counsel, if you can't afford a lawyer, one will be appointed for you.

If you choose, you may have a lawyer during
interrogation. You are accused of having
poisoned and killed your father.
- You are crazy.
- No, I am not crazy.

He put his hand in one of the coat's pockets and
extracted a phial of arsenic.
- Do you know what this is?
- No, I don't.
- This is a phial of arsenic. You can smell it too.
  It has the same smell as the bottle.
- Why have you taken my coat?
- We had to register the house. This is a crime
  scene.
- This is ridiculous; I have not killed my father.
- I'm sorry, but the evidence is clear.
- Anyone could have put the phial there.
- Yes, but the fact is that it was in your coat.
- I am innocent! , I am innocent! , John shouted
  desperately.

He looked at me when they were taking him to
prison and said:
- Would you like to be my lawyer?
- Yes, John, I am going to be your lawyer.

A few minutes later I was at the prison and I was
able to see my client, but I phoned my wife first and
told her to come to London the following day. When
I saw John he was very sad. I tried to calm him
down and then I asked him.
- Well John, let's go straight to the point.
- What point?
- Have you killed your father?
- No, sir I have not killed him, he answered
  surprised for the question.
- That's all I needed to know.
- What is going to happen now?
- Now we are going to discover the truth.
- How?

- I don't know it yet. First, I will come tomorrow morning and you will have to tell me all you have done today.
- I will do it, sir.
- I know you will. See you tomorrow.

When I was leaving the cell, John told me:
- Could you do me a favour?
- Yes, what do you want?
- I want you to tell my brother to phone my wife and tell her what has happened.
- You can do it yourself; you are allowed to do a telephone call.
- I prefer not to do it. My eldest daughter is only five years old and I don't want her to hear that her father is in prison.
- I understand. I will do it.
- Thank you.
- You are welcome. Now try to sleep.
- I will try to do it sir, thank you.
- You are welcome.

One minute later I left the prison and looked for a hotel to spend the night or nights which were going to come. It had been a very hard and terrible day and I needed to have some sleep and a clear mind because I had to defend a man who had been accused of having killed his father, and I still did not know how I was going to do it. It had been a long time since the last time I had defended a person accused of having committed a crime.

CHAPTER 2: JOHN BROWN

The autopsy revealed what I already knew. John had been murdered. The arsenic caused his death. When I knew that I went to the prison to talk to my client. When I entered he looked at me. I could see from the very first moment the sadness in his eyes. When I saw him I noticed he had not slept. He looked very tired and worried.

- Good morning, I said.
- Good morning, he answered.
- Have you slept well?
- No, I haven't. I don't know why my father has been killed and why I am here.
- Neither do I, but don't worry we are going to discover the truth and the real murderer or murderers are going to pay for what they have done.
- Murderers? Do you think there is more than one?
- Maybe, that is what we have to guess. But in order to do that, I have to know exactly what you did yesterday, why you came here and who do you think could be interested in killing your father.
- I thought no one.
- If anyone could be interested in killing your father he wouldn't be dead.
- Yes, I suppose he wouldn't.
- Why did you come here yesterday?
- Because he wanted to talk to us.
- About what?
- About the will.
- Why?
- Because he thought he was going to die soon.
- I see. Who inherited all his fortune?
- My brother and me, one half for each one.
- When did you arrive at your father's house?

- We arrived at one o'clock to have lunch with him.
- Who opened the door?
- The maid.
- Did you give her your coat?
- Yes, I did, but when I took it two hours later, there was nothing in my pocket.
- Where did she put your coats?
- She put them in the cupboard that is at the entrance, where the police found them.
- What did you do after she opened the door?
- We waited for our father, said hello and gave him the bottle of whisky.
- Did he open it?
- Yes, after lunch.
- Where were you?
- First, we were in the living room, and then we went to the library.
- How long did you stay there?
- Half an hour more or less.
- Did your father bring the bottle to the library?
- No, he didn't.
- So the bottle stayed half an hour alone on the table.
- Yes.
- Were the three of you all the time in the library?
- No, Charles was five minutes out of the library.
- Why?
- Because he went to the toilet.
- Was he only five minutes out?
- Yes, he was.

He stared at me, and one minute later he said.
- Listen, my brother wouldn't even think of killing my father, we loved our father so much.

- I am not blaming him, don't worry. I have another question, why did you leave home yesterday?
- Because we went to visit some friends. We told our father we would be back one hour before dinner.
- When you returned, who opened the door?
- Edward the butler.
- Did you give him the coats?
- Yes, we did.
- What did he do with them?
- He put them in the cupboard.
- I think I will have to talk to him.
- Do you think he killed my father?
- Maybe.
- I can't believe he could have killed our father. He has been working for him during more than twenty-five years, first with his wife, but she died two years ago.
- What was the cause of her death?
- She had cancer.
- What did he do later?
- He wanted to leave the house and the country and move to Scotland, but my father did not allow him to do it.
- Why?
- Because he wanted him to stay with him.
- So, he had a good reason to kill your father.
- That is not a strong motive.
- Maybe not but....
- Anyone could have put the phial in my pocket.
- Yes, but that person should have known where the coat was, and he knew it.
- But the other people in the house also knew where the coats were.
- Yes, but...
- So, that reduces the list of suspects to someone from the house.
- Yes.

- But who? Many people have been working for my father for many years.
- I do not know; that's what I will try to discover.
- How did that person obtain the poison?
- He or she could have bought and hidden it.

I remained silent for a moment and then I asked to my client:
- At what time did you leave the house?
- We had lunch at one, left the house at three, and went back at six, when we met you.
- Yes, I know. Ok, that is all for the moment. I will come this afternoon.
- Thanks.
- You are welcome.

He looked at me and, after a moment asked me.
- Could you do me a favour?
- Of course.
- My wife comes today by train. Could you go with my brother to pick her up to Paddington station?
- Yes, of course, don't worry about anything.
- Thank you very much.
- You are welcome.

I turned around and left the prison.

CHAPTER 3: CHARLES BROWN

Before going to meet Linda at the station I went to John's house, and Charles was there. He was tall, a dark-haired man and strong. One could imagine from the beginning that he was a teacher. He liked reading, especially; of course, chemistry books, and he also had the same hobby as his father. He liked poisons, that is why he discovered at the very first moment by the smell that it was arsenic what had killed his father.

When I met him, he told me.

- I have phoned Linda, her train arrives at Paddington station in 30 minutes, we can go with my car, if you want.
- All right.

He seemed very nervous and anxious. I suppose that should be normal, because his brother was in prison accused of having committed a murder of which he was innocent, and his father had been killed and he had no idea why.

- I cannot believe this may be happening, my father is dead and my brother is accused of having killed him. All this is a nightmare.
- Yes, it is, but it will finish soon.
- Do you have any suspect?
- Not at the moment.
- I hope the murderer pays for what he or she has done.
- Murder or murderers.
- Do you think there is more than one?
- I am still thinking about that, but yes, that is a possibility.
- I still can't believe it.
- Neither can I. By the way, can I ask you a question?
- Of course.
- Your brother has told me that after lunch you were half an hour with your father at the library,

but you were out there five minutes, is that correct?.
- Yes, that's right, I went to the toilet.
- Anywhere else?
- What do you mean? Do you think I went to the living room, put the poison in the bottle and the phial of arsenic in my brother's coat?
- No, I don't, but I asked myself if you could tell me something that could be useful for my investigations.
- Like what?
- I don't know. Did you see or hear anything when you went to the toilet?
- No, I didn't.

He started thinking and one minute later said:
- Oh yes! I heard something, although I think it is not important.
- I will say if it is important or not, can you tell me what you heard?
- I heard Edward the butler saying in a loud voice for Christ's sake, hurry up!
- Do you know to whom he was talking?
- I don't know, I suppose to the cooker. I gave no importance to it, sometimes they delay preparing the dinner.
- I consider this extremely important. We have to know to whom he was talking and about what they were talking.

Five minutes later we arrived at Paddington Station, the train arrived on time, and Linda Donaldson got off it.

CHAPTER 4: LINDA DONALDSON

Linda Donaldson was blond; she had big blue eyes, long legs and was tall. She had a soft skin, and a deep look. She had very soft hands. She had a very sweet smile. She was Swedish. She was born in a small village near Stockholm. She grew up there, but when she was twenty she moved to England. She started working as a model, and she had a lot of success in her career. One year later she had moved to England, she met John. It was love at first sight. They started dating and three years later they got married. The first two years they lived in London, but then they moved to Liverpool.

She was a very good model. She was very pretty and, at the same time, she was also very polite and friendly. She spoke English very well.

This time she was very nervous. She could not understand at all why her husband had been arrested. She told me almost crying:

- I just cannot believe this can happen to us. My husband is a very honest and decent man who loved his father so much. He cannot have killed him.
- Don't worry, try to stay calm. I have already talked to your husband. He has told me he has not killed his father and I believe him.
- Thank you Mr Smith. I know you believe him and you are going to help us.
- Of course I am going to help you.
- There is one thing I don't understand.
- Which one?
- Why has he been arrested?
- Because the police have found a phial of arsenic in his coat's pocket.
- Yes, that is what Charles was telling me by the phone, but that is ridiculous, he did not know anything about poisons.

- No, but someone did and introduced a phial of arsenic in his coat so that the police found it there and arrested him.
- But who and why?
- I don't know, but I will discover the answers to your questions. But now, do you want to see your husband?
- Yes, of course.
- Then we will drive you to prison and you will be able to see him.
- Thank you very much.
- You are welcome.

Twenty minutes later we were at the prison. When we entered John went towards his wife and hugged and kissed her.

- Don't worry darling, Mike is a very good lawyer and we are going to win. He is going to discover who the real murderer is. Now, how are our children?
- They are fine, they are with my parents. They are going to be with them until all this ends.

She started crying. Her husband hugged and kissed her softly on her lips.

- Hey, don't cry my love, I am innocent, I have not killed anybody, and Mike is going to prove it. Trust me.
- I trust you.
- Now Charles is going to drive you to the hotel.
- Ok darling.

When Charles and Linda went out I stayed in the cell talking to my client. He started telling me:

- She is so sweet. I'm so sorry for her.

He sighed and looked at me without saying anything. One minute later, he said:

- We are going to win, aren't we?
- Yes, we are, but we have to work hard in order to prove you are innocent.
- And discover the real murderers.

- Of course.
- Do you have any clue?
- No, I don't. Do you have any idea of who could have done it?
- No, I don't. I still can't believe anyone could have thought of killing my father.
- Anyone benefits from his death?
- No one.
- Anyone must have benefited or he wouldn't be dead, what we have to ask for ourselves is to whom and why.
- But who can have benefited?
- I don't know at the moment.
- What are you going to do now?
- I am going to the house and ask the butler and the maid.
- Do you think one of them could have killed my father?
- I don't know, that is what I will try to guess.
- I can't believe Edward can be a murderer.
- What about Mary?
- I don't know, she started working for my father one year ago. I don't think she can be a murderer; she's so young and sweet.
- No one can be considered a murderer until he or she kills someone for the first time.
- Good thought.
- Thank you. By the way, did you father have problems with anyone?
- The day before the murder he had had a heated discussion with his editor. My father wanted to work for another editorial.
- Yes, I know, I suppose the editor wouldn't allow it.
- I suppose he wouldn't.
- Thank you very much John. If you remember anything else, please tell me, I will come tomorrow.
- Thank you Mike.

- You are welcome.
  I went out from the cell and left the prison.

CHAPTER 5: EDWARD THE BUTLER

When I arrived at the house, Edward the butler opened the door. He was about fifty-nine years old. He was bald and wore glasses. He was Scottish. He was born in Edinburgh. I had already met him before when I had come the last time to London to visit John. He had always been loyal to him. He was now a widower. His wife had died two years before, just the same year John's wife died. When I rang the bell he opened the door. He had a sad look in his eyes. He told me.

- It is very sad. Mr Brown is dead and John is in prison.
- Yes it is terrible.

During one minute there was an intense silence. I entered and sat on a chair. He asked me:

- Would you like anything to drink, sir?
- No, thanks, I only want you to answer me a couple of questions.
- Whatever you want, sir.
- First of all, you are not English, are you?
- No sir, I am Scottish.
- That is what I thought.
- I am from Edinburgh.
- It's a lovely city.
- Have you ever been there, sir?
- Yes, once. It's very nice.
- And the whole of Scotland.
- Why did you come here to London?
- Because I wanted to travel a little. I came to London, I met my wife here and two years later we got married.
- How old were you?
- I was 28 and my wife was 25.
- And she died two years ago, didn't she?
- Yes, she had cancer.
- And one year after you got married you started working for Mr Brown, didn't you?

- Yes, we had been working in other houses and one year before the wedding we knew Mr Brown needed people and we came here.
- What was the job of your wife?
- She was the maid.
- Oh yes, she was blond, blue eyes.
- And friendly, and the most beautiful woman in the world.
- Yes, I remember her now and I also remember that when you introduced yourself it was not the first time we met.
- I didn't remember you sir, but your face seemed familiar to me.

We both remained silent for a few seconds and then I asked:

- Did you and your wife have children?
- No, sir we hadn't, we tried, but she aborted three times.
- Oh, that's terrible, I'm sorry.
- Thank you.
- I suppose you felt very sad after your wife's death.
- Yes, I got very depressed.
- And I suppose Mr Brown..?.
- He has always been very good to me, very understanding, but when she died I got very depressed and wanted to leave England and move to Scotland.
- And what happened?
- He did not allow me to leave the house.
- Why?
- Because he wanted me to stay with him. He said I was like a brother for him, and a friend. Moreover his wife had died one month before.
- How was your relationship with him during these 30 years?
- Very good sir, I loved him so much.
- And after your wife's death?
- Very normal, sir.

- What are you going to do now that Mr Brown is dead?
- I will go back to Scotland.
- So, Mr Brown's death has allowed you to move to Scotland, hasn't it?
- What do you mean? , what are you trying to say?
- How did you feel when he did not allow you to move to Scotland?
- At the beginning I was very disappointed, but then...
- Then?
- I realised he did not want me to move because I was like a brother for him. I would never have thought of killing him.
- I am not saying that, don't worry. Did you know if Mr Brown had enemies?
- No, sir I don't think so, he was a wonderful person.
- Could you tell me anything about the day of the murder?
- Like what?
- Whatever you think that could be very useful for me.
- I don't know what could be useful for you.
- Let's see. Mr Brown had a visit the day before, right?
- Yes, the editor, Harry came and they had a heated discussion because Mr Brown wanted to work for another editor.
- But he did not come the day of the murderer didn't he?
- No, he didn't
- Who came that day?
- Let me think, the postman brought a letter for Mr Brown.
- Anyone else?
- Jason Parker, the neighbour came because he wanted to talk to Mr Brown.

- Do you know what he wanted to talk to Mr
  Brown for?
- No, sir.
- I see, is Jason Parker the one who lives next
  door?
- Yes, at number fifteen.
- Did you open the door to him?
- Yes, I did.
- Who opened the door to his sons the day of
  the murderer when they came for the second
  time?
- I opened it, sir.
- While I was talking to Mr Brown at the
  library, is that right?
- Yes it is.
- What did you do with the coats?
- I put them in the cupboard next to the
  entrance.
- Where the police found them.
- Yes, sir.

I stayed during one minute with a lost look, looking
at him. He woke me up from my thoughts and said:
- Excuse me sir, do you have more questions? I
  still have a lot of work to do.
- No, I don't have more questions, you can go.
- Thank you, sir.

He stood up and when he was leaving the room I
said in a loud voice:
- Oh!, Yes, I almost forgot, I have one final
  question, the day of the murderer Charles
  Brown heard you saying in a loud voice "For
  Christ sake, hurry up!" Who were you talking
  to?

While we were talking, Mary Robertson, the maid,
entered into the room.
- He was talking to us. We had delayed a little
  with the dinner.
- I see. Could I ask you a few questions?
- Of course, sir.

- If you don't want anything else, I will continue with my work, Edward said.
- Yes, you can go, thank you.
He stood up and left the room.

CHAPTER 6: MARY ROBERTSON

Mary Robertson was not very tall; she had dark hair and big green eyes. She was only twenty-three.
- I think I have never met you before, where were you born?
- I was born here in London.
- Have you lived all your life here?
- Yes, I have.
- Do you have parents or family?
- No, I haven't, they died in a car accident when I was five years old.
- Don't you have more family, like grandparents, brethren?
- No, I was an only child. I lived with my aunt until she died three years ago. Then I started working for Mr Brown.
- Haven't you done anything else?
- No, I haven't, I wanted to study and go to the university, but I had no money.
- I see, that's terrible.
- Yes, it is.

She remained silent during one minute, I looked at her. She was nervous. She asked:
- What can I do for you?
- I suppose you know I am investigating Mr Brown's murder.
- Yes, I know that.
- Do you know if Mr Brown had enemies?
- No, I don't think so. He was a very nice person.
- Yes, except for the murderer or murderers.
- Do you think there is more than one?
- Maybe.
- Do you have any idea of who has killed Mr Brown?
- No, I do not.

She remained silent, and then I asked her:
- How was your relationship with Mr Brown?

- Very good sir. He has always taken care of me. He knew I was an orphan and he has always helped me.
- Did he offer you money to go to the university?
- Yes, sir, but I did not accept it.
- Why?
- Because I did not want another person to pay my studies. I wanted to pay them myself.
- But he wanted to help you.
- Yes, but I would have had a very big debt with him that I would have had to pay sooner or later, and I already had a very big debt with him because he gave me a job.
- I think you were wrong, you should have accepted his help.
- Maybe.
- What are you going to do now?
- I don't know, maybe I will try to find another job and go to the university.
- That would be a very good idea, what would you like to study?
- Chemistry.

She remained silent and I asked her:
- The day of the murder Edward opened the door to John and Charles Brown the second time, is that correct?
- Yes, it is.
- He says he put the coats in the cupboard where the police found them.
- Yes, that's right.
- Did you see what he did with the coats?
- What do you mean?
- I mean if you saw him putting something inside one of the coats when he hung them.
- Do you think Edward killed Mr Brown?
- Maybe.
- But that's ridiculous what reasons could he have to kill Mr Brown?

- When her wife died he wanted to go back to Scotland and Mr Brown said no.
- Because Mr Brown loved Edward so much. Moreover that is not a strong reason.
- Maybe not, did you see or hear anything?
- No, sir, I did not.
- Ok, that's all for the moment.
- Thank you sir.

She stood up and left the room.

CHAPTER 7: JASON PARKER

When I finished talking to Mary Robertson, I went to visit Jason Parker. As Edward the butler had told me, he was Mr Brown's neighbour. Although he couldn't tell me, I knew later that Mr Parker had started living there half a year ago. He was tall, strong, brown and curly hair, green eyes and a big nose. When I rang the bell, he opened the door, and I noticed immediately his surprise at seeing me standing up there.

- Good morning.
- Good morning, my name is Mike Smith.
- Were you one of John Brown's friends?
- Yes, I was.
- I saw you at the funeral.
- Can I come in?
- Yes, of course.
- Thank you.

The living room was very big; there was a library at the front, a table with four chairs on the right and two sofas on the left side. The bedrooms were on the first floor. There was not too much decoration, and there were no photos, only one abstract painting on one wall.

- What could I do for you?
- I am investigating John Brown's murder.
- Are you a policeman?
- No, I'm not, I am a lawyer. His son John has been accused of having killed his father.
- Excuse me, I have forgotten offering, do you want a drink?
- No, thank you.
- I am going to pour one for myself.
- As you wish.
- So you are John Brown's lawyer?
- Yes, that's right.
- So, what do you want to know?

- Edward has told me that the day of the murderer you went to John Brown's house, is that right?
- Yes, it is. I went to ask him if he could give me a book to read.
- Did he give it to you?
- Yes, he did.
- This one over here?
- Yes.
- Did you like it?
- Yes, I did.
- May I borrow it?
- Yes, I was going to give it back to Mr Brown the following day.
- I will give it back for you.
- Thanks.
- What do you think about John Brown's death?
- He has always taken care of the people, I still can't believe he had been killed, and by his own son!
- He hasn't killed his father, and I am going to prove it.
- But he has been arrested.
- Yes, I know, but I am going to demonstrate his innocence and I am going to arrest the real murderers.
- How are you going to do it?
- I'm sorry, but I am not going to tell you.
- I see.
- When did you start living here?
- Six months ago. I was working in the Natural History Museum, but then I decided to move here because I had found a job in the British Museum. They paid me more money.
- What is your job?
- I am one of the guards of the museum.
- Where did you live when you worked in the National History Museum?
- I was living in Kensington road.

- I see. How old are you, if I may ask you?
- I am twenty-three.
- Where were you born?
- I was born in Cambridge.
- When did you come here?
- When I was ten.
- Did you go to the university?
- No, I did not, my family was poor, my mother died when I was fifteen, and my father when I was seventeen, then I started living with my aunt, but she died when I was twenty.
- Oh, I'm sorry.
- Thanks.
- What did you do later?
- I started working in different jobs, always hired and going from one place to another.
- Do you have any brother or sister?
- No, I do not.
- Ok thanks.That´s all for the moment.
- It has been nice to talk to you. If you need something else, please, tell me.
- Thanks, I will do it.

I stood up and went out.

CHAPTER 8: HARRY WHITEHALL

That afternoon I went to visit the editor, who was called Harry Whitehall. When I arrived, his secretary introduced me.

- Mr Whitehall, there is one man here who says he is Mike Smith; he is the lawyer of Mr Brown. He wants to talk to you.
- Tell him to come in.
- Yes sir.
- Mr Brown, you can come in, Mr Whitehall is waiting for you.
- Thank you, Mrs Jefferson.

When I saw him for the first time I noticed he was a typical English man, with his umbrella, his hat, a photo of his wife and his children and a half drunk cup of tea on the table. He was tall; he had dark hair and brown eyes. He was fifty-five years old, but he seemed younger.When I entered he came towards me and said:

- Hi, nice to meet you! My name is Harry Whitehall; I am the owner of this editorial.
- Hi, my name is Mike Smith, I am a lawyer and I am investigating Mr Brown's death.
- Have you discovered anything?
- Not at the moment.
- Excuse me I have not offered you anything to drink; do you want a cup of tea?
- No, thanks.
- So, you were saying?
- Mr Brown was a friend of mine.
- I see what can I do for you?
- The day before the murder you went to John Brown's house, is that true?
- Yes, It is.
- Why?
- Because he wanted to talk to me.
- About what?

- About his new book. He told me he would delay a little.
- What did you tell him?
- I told him not to worry. He could send it when he had it ready. After all he had been working for us for more than thirty years, so if he delayed a little it would be no problem for us.
- Yes, but you demanded too much to him.
- He had become very passive. I only told him to write.
- That's why he wanted to go to another editorial.
- That's not true.
- Why didn't you offer him more money?
- Because his books were not so good as before.
- What would happen if he left your editorial?
- We would lose a great sum of money.
- And you wouldn't allow that, would you?
- Excuse me?
- Do you know what I think?
- What do you think?
- I think he was tired of you because you pressed him, that's why he wanted to go to another editorial, but you were not going to permit that, so what you did was to threaten him. You had a very strong motive to kill him, and in fact you killed him.
- How do you dare? , how can you come here to my office and insult me? I was not at the house that day; his son killed him. I did not poison him.
- Maybe not, but...
- Get out of here!
- See you at the trial.

I stood up, said goodbye and left the room.

CHAPTER 9: THE TRIAL

Finally, the day of the trial arrived. I had made a list of suspects who could have killed Mr Brown.

1- His son Charles. If his father died and his brother was guilty of the murder, he would inherit all the fortune.
2- His maid, not very likely.
3- His butler, when his wife died he wanted to return to Scotland and Mr Brown did not allow it.
4- His editor.Mr Brown had told him he would go to another editor. They had a big discussion the day before the murder.
5- His neighbour. Not very likely.

At 11:30 the trial started. The plaintive was called George Edwards. The first witness of the prosecution was the police inspector.

He said that in the bottle they analysed, they had found arsenic at the bottom, and they had found a phial of arsenic in John's coat. When it was my turn I asked him:

- Mr Johnson, did you find fingerprints of my customer in the phial you found in his coat?
- No, sir.
- Thank you sergeant. I have no more questions.
- You can go.

The accusation calls the doctor Frank Robertson.

- Doctor, what was the cause of Mr Brown's death?
- He was killed by the effects of arsenic found in the cup of whisky he had drunk.
- Thank you, doctor. No more questions. It is your turn Mr Smith.
- Thank you Mr Edwards. Doctor, in the morning of the murder, when you went to see your patient, how did he feel?
- Not very well because he had broken with his editor although, on the other hand, he felt well because his sons were going to visit him.

- And physically?
- Not very well, he smoked and drank a lot, and his health was getting worse.
- Do you think Mr Brown knew he was going to die soon?
- Yes, I think so. I found him very pessimistic.
- I see. Doctor, do you know John and Charles?
- Yes I do.
- Do you think any of them would kill their father to get his fortune?
- Objection.
- Granted.
- There are no more questions, thank you, doctor.

The accusation calls the accused John Brown to the witness box.

- Mr Brown, Do you think that the relationship between you, your father and your brother could be considered as normal?
- Yes, absolutely.
- But, has your father ever been out of his mind and threatened you or your brother?
- No.
- Sure? , remember you are on oath now, has your father ever threatened you or your brother?
- Oh! That was a stupid thing.
- Answer the question straight to the point please, yes or no?
- Yes, once.
- What did he say?
- He said that we were very lazy, that we were not very good sons and that at the end he would disinherit us.
- So you wished to kill your father, in fact you killed him because he was going to disinherit you and your brother didn't you?
- No, I didn't, I loved my father! , John said in a loud voice.

- Objection.
- Granted.
- I withdraw the question. There are no more questions.It´s the time of the defence.
- Thank you Mr Edwards, John, you and your brother gave your father a bottle as a present the day of the murderer, is that correct?
- Yes, it is.
- Did he open it?
- Yes, he did.
- Where were you?
- We were at the living room.
- Did you stay there all the time?
- No, we were there after lunch, and then we went to the library.
- Why did you go to the library?
- Because my father wanted to talk to us.
- About what?
- About the testament.
- Did your father take the bottle with him?
- No, he didn't.
- Where did he put it?
- He put it on the table that is in the living room.
- So, anyone could have put the arsenic in the bottle while you were in the library, is this true?
- Objection.
- Granted.
- I withdraw the question. I only have one more question to the witness. John, when your father threatened you and your brother and said he would disinherit you, how old were you?
- I was ten and my brother was eight.
- Only ten! And how old are you now?
- I'm forty-five.
- So, that was thirty-five years ago! , so one must have cruel feelings if he wants to kill his

own father for something this said thirty-five
years ago, that is no serious, for Christ sake,
you were only ten years old !.
I stopped, took a deep breath, looked to my client
and asked him.
- Mr Brown, Did you have malice against your
  father for what he said thirty-five years ago?
- No, I did not.
- Did you kill him?
- No, I did not, I loved my father.
- Thank you John there is no more questions.
- The prosecution has already finished with its
  witnesses.
- Now it's time of the defence, you can call to
  your first witness.
- The defence calls Charles Brown.
- Charles, the day of the murder you stayed
  during five minutes outside the library alone, is
  that correct?
- Yes, it is, I went to the toilet.
- Did you hear anything?
- Yes, I heard Edward was telling For Christ's
  sake, hurry up! to someone.
- Do you know to whom he was talking?
- No, I don't.
- Thank you Charles, there are no more
  questions. It's the time of the prosecution.
- There are no questions.
After that, the trial was suspended until the
following day. That night I was thinking on the case,
I had a theory and I thought I could prove it, I knew
I couldn't be wrong. Finally, I told it to my wife.
- I 've got it! I have the solution to the case.

CHAPTER 10: ALL THE TRUTH

The next morning the trial started at 10:00. I called
Edward the butler. I noticed he was not at the court.
I said again:
- The defence calls Edward McDonald.
The constable went to the room outside and
shouted his name twice but he did not appear. The
judge said:
- Mr Smith, if your witness is not here in one
  minute you will have to call another witness.
- I'm sorry, your honour. The defence asks for
  five minutes break to discover where the
  witness is.
- The accusation objects.
- Granted. Mr Smith, if you can't control your
  witnesses that is not our responsibility. You
  will have to call another witness.
Suddenly my wife, who had gone out to phone and
discover where the butler was, entered and told me
something which froze my heart. I stayed a minute
looking at her with horror eyes without knowing
what to say, whereas the judge went on talking to
me and asking me questions. I could not imagine
Edward was going to be killed; his murder was a
nasty surprise for me. One minute later I woke up
from my dreams and I heard the judge telling me:
- Lawyer, you will have to call the next witness.
  If you don't have any the trial will have
  finished and the jury will go to decide.
- Your honour! The defence asks for one hour
  break. Edward McDonald has been found at
  the house dead with a shot in his head.
- Objection.
- Accepted.
- Your honour, can I approach?
- Yes, you can, and the prosecutor as well.

- Your honour, Edward Mc Donald is a vital
  testimony for the defence, and he has been
  killed.
- We did not know that, and that is a tragedy,
  but the process must continue, your honour.
- I agree with the prosecution, there is not going
  to be one hour break, the request is rejected.
- Thank you your honour.
- But…
- I'm sorry, call your next witness or this
  process will be finished.

I gave a quick look at the public and at the faces of
the people. After one minute I returned to my desk,
raised my head, looked at the front and said in a
loud and clear voice:

- The defence calls Mary Robertson to the
  witness box.

She stood up, passed next to me and went to the
witness box. The bailiff said:

- Raise your right hand.
- Do you swear to tell the truth, all the truth and
  nothing but the truth?
- Yes, I do.
- Could you tell your name please?
- Mary Robertson.
- You can sit down.
- Thanks.

Then I started with my questions.

- Miss Robertson, where were you born?
- I was born here in London
- When?
- In 1974.
- Do you have family, Miss Robertson?
- No, I haven't. My parents died in a car
  accident when I was five years old.
- Do you have any brother or sister?
- No, I haven't.
- No? are you sure?
- Yes, I am.

- All right, you say you are sure you don't have a brother, but I tell you that you have one.
- What?
- Do you recognise that man over there?
- Yes, he is Mr Brown's neighbour.
- But the relation you have with him is closer than a simple neighbour, is that right?
- I don't know what you mean.
- Of course you know what I mean!

I took one photo from my table and shew it to her.

- Miss Robertson, Do you recognise this photo?

She could not say anything when she saw the photo. She appeared with her brother, who was Mr Brown's neighbour, the man sat among the public.

- Is it true that he is your brother and that your real name is Susan Jordan?

She was really surprised when she saw the photo and when she heard her real name. She did not know what to say. She looked many times at the photo and at me. After one minute I asked her:

- Is he your brother, yes or no?
- Ok, yes, he is my brother, and my real name is Susan Jordan.
- Are you and your brother twins?
- Yes, we are.
- Isn't it true that your father abandoned you, your brother and your mother before you were born and then your mother deserted you because she could not take care of you?
- Yes, it is.
- And you both went to an orphanage, didn't you?
- Yes, we did.
- And you escaped from there when you were twenty.
- Yes.
- And when you escaped you killed a man in order to survive.
- No, we didn't.

- No? I know you did, and I can prove it. The case appeared on the newspapers and on TV, and I can show you one newspaper I have here where says that a girl and a boy had killed a banker of an important bank of London and had stolen his wallet.

She sighed, looked at her brother, then to the floor, and finally to me.

- The girl and the boy are you and your brother, is that true?
- Yes, it is.
- What happened then?
- We were arrested two days later.
- What happened after that?
- The trial was celebrated and we were sent to prison.
- And the witness of the prosecution was Mr Brown, wasn't he?
- Yes, he was. He recognised us.
- And two years later you escaped from prison.
- Yes.
- What happened then?
- We disappeared and changed our names and our physical aspect.
- And one year ago you started working for Mr Brown, didn't you?
- Yes, I did.
- Why?
- Because we wanted to revenge on the person who had sent us to prison.
- And you thought that after three years and with a different aspect he would not recognise you.
- Well, he did not recognise me, but he started asking me questions about my past, and I thought he would discover the truth sooner or later.
- What did you do?

- I phoned my brother and half a year ago he moved next to Mr Brown's house and we planned the murder.
- And you did it quite well, but you committed a mistake.
- Yes, we didn't take you into account.
- You neither did with Edward; he was going to tell all the truth today.
- That's why my brother has killed him.
- So, Edward did not agree with all this plan of killing Mr Brown didn't he?
- No, he didn't. He wanted to kill him two years ago when his wife died and Mr Brown did not allow him to leave the house and we knew that, so we threatened him of telling the whole story to Mr Brown.
- But he could also have told Mr Brown what your past was and your plan.
- That was a risk we had to run. Anyway, Mr Brown was going to die sooner or later, and if he said something he would die as well.

I remained silent for one minute staring at her and then I asked:
- By the way when he said for Christ sake, hurry up! It had nothing to do with the dinner, is that true?
- No it had not. He told me to hurry up when I was going to introduce the arsenic in the bottle because we could get caught.
- But you did not introduce the poison in the bottle nor the phial in John's pocket then.
- No, I introduced the poison in the bottle and the phial in John's pocket while the four of you were in the library and Edward entered to tell you that dinner was served.
- So when he went out from the library, entered into the living room, took the bottle and poured himself another glass for the dinner you had already introduced the poison in the bottle.

- Yes, that's right.

I looked and asked her.

- The editor Harry Whitehall is the accomplice, is that right?
- No, he isn't.
- No? Of course he is! He bought the arsenic and gave it to your brother the day of the murder didn't he?
- Yes he did.
- One final question why did you introduce the phial in John's pocket?
- I did not know who the owner of the coat was, I only opened the cupboard and introduced it in the coat I had nearer.
- So, you could also have put it in my coat.
- Yes, I think that was our big mistake. I should have put it in your coat, so you would have been accused of killing Mr Brown.
- You would not have got your own way. Sooner or later the police would have captured you.
- You are very sure of what you are saying.
- Yes, I am. Your past would have captured you sooner or later and in fact has. By the way, you told me that you would have a big debt with Mr Brown, and that's right, with his murder you will have a big debt with him forever because you will never be able to pay your freedom.

I stayed during a few seconds staring at her, into her eyes. After that I looked at the judge and said:

- Your honour, the defence wishes that all the charges against my client John Brown be withdrawn immediately and to put Miss Susan Jordan, her brother James Jordan and the editor Harry Whitehall under arrest.
- The prosecution agrees.
- All the charges against John Brown have been withdrawn. The hearing is over. Put Susan Jordan, her brother and the editor under arrest.

When the judge said these words my client told me:
- Thank you very much. You have saved my life. I don't know how I can pay you for all you have done for me.
- It is nothing; I was only doing my job.
- Thank you for everything, Linda said.
- Don't mention it.

After that my wife told me.
- I am astonished; you have solved a very difficult case.
- Yes, but not without your help.
- Thank you darling. When did you start to realise she was the murderer?
- When I saw her brother. They are very similar. When I saw him, I realised I had already seen that face before.
- Why did they kill that man?
- Well, their parents were wanderers, their father abandoned their mother when she was pregnant and she abandoned them after they were born. They were sent to an orphanage and they escaped when they were twenty. Then they killed the man because they needed money to survive.
- And then they were captured, weren't they?
- Yes, the photos of the criminals appeared in the newspapers and they were sent to prison, but they escaped.
- What happened later?
- They changed their names and their physical aspect. The police looked for but did not find them.
- I could not recognise any of them.
- I have to admit that I did not recognise her, three years before she was blond and now she was dark-haired and she had operated her nose.
- But you recognised him.
- Yes, I did.

- Why didn't they go to another country when they escaped from prison?
- Because the police broadcasted their photos to other countries and they were safe nowhere. On the other hand, they had no money and they wanted to revenge from the person who had sent them to prison.
- And that person was Mr Brown.
- Yes, he declared during the trial that he had seen two people killing a man and stealing him the wallet.
- And when she started working for him he did not know she was the person he had sent to prison.
- Neither that his neighbour was the other person.
- So they prepared his murder, and he had no idea someone wanted to kill him.
- Yes, that's right. He did not know that his maid and his neighbour were the two people he had sent to prison some years ago and that was his death penalty. They had hidden for some time and then they decided to revenge. She started to work for Mr Brown one year ago. They thought they were safe. He was working and living in Kensington road, but when Mr Brown started to ask her questions about her past, she started to be afraid of him, so she phoned his brother, who hired a house next to his half a year ago and they decided to put their plan into action.
- So, they plannified the murder quite well.
- Yes, they did.
- So, He was condemned.
- Yes, he was.
- What kind of questions did Mr Brown ask her?
- I don't know, but I think he thought his maid could be the person he had sent to prison some

years before. He wanted to know more things about her past because her face seemed familiar to him.
- Why didn't he phone the police?
- I think he could not imagine that his friendly maid could be the person to whom he sent to prison neither could he imagine that his neighbour was his brother. He thought he was wrong.
- But he wasn't.
- No, he wasn't.
- What happens with the two different stories they told you?
- All lies.
- I see, and, if she had been working for him during one year, why didn't they..?.
- Why didn't they try to kill him earlier?
- Yes.
- In fact they tried, one day he broke Mr Brown's break's car, another day she poisoned his food with cyanide, another day he shot him but he only hurt him in his arm, and finally one day he tried to push him from the eleventh floor from a hotel.
- And he did not know anyone wanted to kill him!
- I think he suspected someone wanted or had tried to kill him, although he did not tell me because he had not proves.
- How did you discover he suspected that anyone had wanted to kill him?
- Because that day he was very nervous and, although his sons had gone to see him, he had a sad look in his eyes, and I knew he was worried about something.
- Why did he not say anything to you?
- Because he did not want to worry me. On the other hand he was not sure of that.Oh, if I had known it!

- You could not know it unless he told you.
- Yes, I suppose so, but....
- Well, at the end we have made justice.Mr Brown would be very happy.
- Yes, he would, although unfortunately he is not here.
- But we are, so why don't we go to celebrate our victory with our children and grandchildren?
- Yes, that is an excellent idea, darling.

So, we took the train to Manchester and celebrated our triumph with our children.